Published by
Princeton Architectural Press
202 Warren Street
Hudson, New York 12534
www.papress.com

First published in France under the title: *Gaspard dans la nuit*
© 2020, De La Martinière Jeunesse, a division
of La Martinière Groupe, Paris

English Edition © 2022 Princeton Architectural Press
All rights reserved.
Printed and bound in China
25 24 23 22   4 3 2 1 First edition

ISBN 978-1-64896-070-3

This book was illustrated using watercolors and colored pencils.

For Princeton Architectural Press:
Editors: Amy Novesky and Stephanie Holstein
Typesetting: Paula Baver

Library of Congress Control Number: 2021931170

George and His Nighttime Friends

Seng Soun Ratanavanh

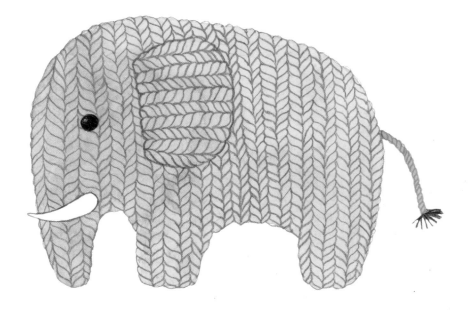

PRINCETON ARCHITECTURAL PRESS

NEW YORK

On a street of snug little houses, under a very cozy roof,
lives a lonely boy named George.

While the rest of the street sleeps nestled in their beds,
George is wide awake. At night, his mind travels.

But even the most wonderful expeditions come to an end.
George slips under his covers, hoping to sleep, or even dream…

Instead, George thinks of his favorite marble, the one he lost.
He thinks of what comes after infinity.
He thinks of monsters that hide in the night.

Did you hear that?!

George is afraid of the dark.
"I wish I had a nighttime friend, even a small one."

In the dark, a voice squeaks,
"Hello, did you call me?"

George cannot believe his eyes or ears!
"No...Yes...I'm—"

"You are looking for a nighttime friend," Mouse says. "Follow me."

George follows Mouse down the stairs and freezes.
Something is moving in the shadows!

"Don't be afraid. This is Mole, the guardian of the books."

Upon hearing their footsteps, Mole twirls around.
"Delighted to meet you, George! How can I help?"

"I am looking for a nighttime friend," George whispers.

Mole rushes to the shelves in search of a book.
Selecting one, the little librarian proudly reads:
"There is nothing more precious in the world
than a nighttime friend!"

After Mole opens up another book, this one
about the universe, they hear someone playing
the piano in the living room.

An elegant rabbit is practicing for a concert.
"Are you a nighttime friend?" George asks.

Sitting atop a pile of books to reach the piano keys,
Rabbit responds without looking up.
"I am very busy practicing."

The music doesn't sound very good, but George politely listens.
And at the end of the piece, he and Mouse give a round of applause.
Rabbit blushes. "I could do much better if I didn't have stage fright."

Soon they hear a squawk come from the bathroom and discover a tiny fluffy bather, quivering between the sink faucets.

George reaches out to the petite penguin. "Are you cold?"

But Penguin shakes her head: "I am not cold, I am afraid!"

"What are you afraid of?" George asks.

"I am afraid of water…
And jumping…
And the dark…
And spiders…
And snow…
And spinach…
And storms…
…And butterflies."

The nighttime friends understand what it is like to be afraid of something.

After drawing a toasty bath, they all pile into
the tub to show Penguin that everything is okay.

Rabbit impresses everyone with his pencil dive!

Their laughter and shouts echo across the room.
Penguin laughs too and soon joins her new friends.

When the water cools, the nighttime friends head to the
laundry room to find some soft towels to dry off.

Suddenly, a curious panda pops out of the dryer to say hello.

"Do you want to play a game?" Panda asks.
"I dream of becoming a champion badminton player,
  but I don't have anyone to practice with!"

And so the nighttime friends begin a spirited game
of badminton.

George hits the birdie to Mouse.
Mouse hits it to Rabbit.
Rabbit hits it to Penguin.
Penguin hits it to Panda, who jumps up and sends
the birdie flying into the kitchen, which is very
good timing because the friends are very hungry!

George knows there is leftover cake in the refrigerator—
though he is in for a surprise.

Opening the fridge door, he finds a pleased little pig polishing
off the chocolate cake! Just as startled by being discovered,
Pig holds his basket of freshly picked mushrooms tightly.

"Are you also a nighttime friend?" George asks.
Before Pig can answer, the others ask all at once,
"Can you please make us something to eat?"

Pig gathers ingredients and, after making a joyful mess, the nighttime friends gather around, their faces glowing by candlelight, to share a dreamy feast of strawberries and cream and sprinkles.

George looks around at all of his wonderful new friends. Nighttime is not so scary after all!

Before too long, George's eyelids become heavy, and he
begins to yawn. The new friends lead George back upstairs
and tuck him into his very cozy bed, their work done.

Until tomorrow.

"Good night, George."
"Good night, my nighttime friends."